# FUCK
# THE POPE
# BUT
# USE A
# CONDOM

## A Dirty Discovery

George pauses to look up at the large black-and-white photograph of his former tenant: Dixon Thompson recreating Rodin's *The Thinker*, chin on fist, gazing ahead with exaggerated gravitas.

George narrows his eyes, tilts his head, and purses his lips. Then: "Plonker."

"George!"

"Sorry, Marge. I know we shouldn't speak ill of the dead, but I sure didn't like the man. He was a plonker, plain and simple."

His wife sighs. "I know …"

The apartment still smells faintly of incense and … something George would rather not think about. He wrinkles his nose and packs the last stack of books into a cardboard box. Margaret moves to the bedside table and opens the drawer.

She gasps and covers her mouth.

George rushes over. Inside: a purple vibrator, hand-cuffs, lube, and an ungodly amount of condoms.

He shakes his head. "Throw it in the trash."

He returns to the desk and opens the top drawer. A manila envelope sits inside, a handwritten note attached. He frowns, then calls over his shoulder, "Marge, come have a look at this."

She joins him. He holds up the note, and she reads it aloud: "Boy oh boy, you're really not supposed to be here, are you? I suggest you close the drawer and leg it, because I swear to god, if I catch you now, I'll rip out your trachea like a weed and toss it to the winds."

She gives George a wide-eyed look, then continues: "If I'm dead, on the other hand, please be so kind as to get this package to my agent. Details inside. Thanks! Dixon, 29/06/2010."

George opens the envelope and slides out a manuscript.

The title page reads: "FUCK THE POPE BUT USE A CONDOM (or A MAN OF NO ORDINARY CALIBER if publishers are pussies) by Dixon Thompson."

Margaret makes the sign of the cross.

George turns the page and begins to read.

## The Curse of the Conman

Misunderstood. That's what I feel. Not due to any negligence or incompetence on my part. No, no. Of that, I can't be convicted. After all, I am a master of communication. I makes no mistakes. See what I did there? Funny as well.

I've been misunderstood because I intended to be misunderstood. I valiantly plumbed the depths of my self-interest and took the necessary steps to keep the results a secret.

But it comes at a cost, this double life, because a man—and I'm just a man, albeit an extraordinary one—longs to be understood, to be seen for who he truly is. It's the curse of the conman: he can claim many things, but credit isn't one of them.

He doesn't like seeing simpletons like Levi Stavropoulos describe him as "comically ignorant" (the irony!) or a "kind of accidental Moses"—or even just how the populace, in general, considers him a mere normal, upstanding biped, as necessary as cultivating this image might be.

He craves, at the very least, the solace of knowing that his secrets won't go with him to the grave, that when he expels his final breath and a facade of respectability has lost its use, humanity will discover who they had *really* been dealing with.

And that, dear friends, is why I am expelling this ink: to set the record straight, to tell you the true story of how my celebrated debut play came to be, so that hopefully, on one fine Capetonian morning, as hadedas pass overhead, screeching like the Devil's choir, Levi Stavropoulos will choke on his toast.

It makes the notion of my demise slightly more palatable.

## Vixens & Third Wheels

Our story truly begins on a Friday evening back in January, when Cape Town was still up to its eyebrows in summer. There I was, ensconced in the damp belly of The Elephant In The Room with two fellow hacks, James and Heinrich.

As the full moon raised its tangerine face above the ominous silhouette of Devil's Peak, their beer-soaked brains somehow got bogged down in the subject of self-deception.

"I'm telling you," insisted James, "Pol Pot, Hitler, Mao—all of these guys thought of themselves as heroes! Not as mad or cruel. If they had, we wouldn't be talking about them right now. They would've been duds, like actors who can't get it out of their heads that they're acting. It's precisely *because* they thought they were good that they could be so bad. It's precisely *because* they could fool themselves that they could fool others."

"What about someone like Ted Bundy?" said Heinrich. "Have you *seen* his interviews? He knew exactly what he was up to. Didn't change a thing. He just kept killing and loved himself for it."

"An exception to the rule. And can you imagine if he'd thought his behavior was for the greater good? That it was ordained by *god?* Don't pull your face like that!" James snatched up a peanut and flicked it at Heinrich, striking him on the forehead. "It happens! Some of the greatest atroc—"

I was only vaguely listening to these exchanges—I may even have misremembered some of the finer points—and I'll tell you why. My mind was elsewhere, and not just at any old place, but with the face and form of a red-hot bird by the name of Yvonne.

We met two days earlier and hit it off—not quite like flint and steel—but nicely, quite nicely. She had recently arrived from Amsterdam, here to study for a few months, and was sipping an ice-cold caipirinha when I approached her and turned on the old roguish charm.

We kissed, but it was brief and, to my consternation, preceded and followed by giggling, which has a way of unsettling a man and making him unsure of what's what.

Consequently, when I texted her earlier that Friday and heard nothing for hours, I became quite the gloomy little boy. It seemed as if, after all, she wasn't that into me.

Now, don't get the wrong idea. I am no moper. No, sir. When I don't hear back from a bird—an occurrence so rare it's practically a statistical anomaly—I simply phone up another. I am a man with options. But see, this Yvonne, she was a special one. A heart-stopper of note. Long, caramelized legs, blue eyes, flaxen hair, frisky butt. You get the picture.

Accordingly, by the time the conversation at the table turned to Ted Bundy, I quite frankly couldn't give a fuck. The whole thing seemed positively meaningless to me. But it was also at this juncture that my fortunes changed.

As the peanut came to a standstill in front of me, my phone lit up. She had texted back: "Hey! Sorry for the late reply. I'm at Crazy Joe's. Come say hello! :)"

The effect was most remarkable. My spine whipped straight, zinging like a guitar string, and the corners of my mouth stretched into such remote regions of my enviable face that James paused mid-sentence to inquire into the state of my mental health. Such is the power of a beautiful woman, my friend. It's terrifying, really.

Ten minutes later, after a jaunty jog up Long Street, dodging and weaving my way through its mishmash of hookers, pushers, hobos, and drunks, I located her at Crazy Joe's main bar.

I was mesmerized. She wore a ruby-red dress, ending several suggestive inches above the knee, and seemed to be enclosed in a kind of divine aureole, setting her apart from her mediocre Irish pub surroundings.

Unfortunately, and to my immediate misgivings—for I had ample experience of the generally bitter, spiteful nature of third wheels—the same pudgy, sullen-looking appendage who had disfigured Cape Town's club scene two days earlier was next to her. Annette was the name.[*]

She saw me first and exhibited just the slightest facial contraction of loathing and displeasure before turning to Yvonne to inform her of my arrival.

Conceive my joy, dear reader, when, merely minutes removed from feeling as if our time was up, this Dutch tulip, upon seeing me, launched herself into my arms and, casting her eyes upward in the most devilish fashion, squeezed my caboose. I mean, after receiving her text, I took it as confirmation that she craved me in the animal way, but I didn't expect this. Not so early at least. And it only got better …

She continued fondling my David-like ass as I ordered drinks—in my merriment, I even ordered one for Annette—and when we received them, she grabbed my hand and, without so much as a glance at the side-

---

[*] To be fair, she wouldn't have been such an eyesore had she been by herself, or among other burrowing animals; but when juxtaposed with a bird like Yvonne … well, it didn't help.

kick, dragged me through the crowd to a corner booth in the adjoining room. There, she let go of my hand and grabbed my cock. Looking at me giddily, she held onto it a moment longer, then relinquished it and started giving it the old genie-in-a-bottle.

Feeling that an eye for an eye was in order, I reached over and, sliding my hand up between her gleaming, honey-glazed thighs, grabbed her monkey. She gasped and gained an inch or two in height, then lunged at and latched onto my lips, sucking at me like a Death Eater for a few seconds before disengaging with a loud smack, her lips curling into a lecherous smile as she drew away.

I smiled back and, after lingering in the maelstrom of our hot, steamy breath for a few moments, we re-engaged. But then, just as our lips touched, there was a sudden and considerable upheaval in our seat—someone sizable had plopped down beside me. What's more, this person proceeded to tap me on the shoulder.

Naturally, I had to unplug from Yvonne to deal with the issue at hand. Some things a man can ignore, but being tapped on the shoulder by a large primate while making out with a prized female is not one of them. Such a cavalier attitude, while no doubt attractive and debonair, can land you an early funeral.

I turned to face the intruder with a grim expression. As I did so, I expected to come up against the pockmarked features of a bouncer. I mean, it wouldn't have been the first time that one of these uglies put the kibosh on one of my sexual acts. But how wrong I was … And believe me, I wish I wasn't, for what slid into view, dear reader, made the notion of a six-foot gorilla in black polyester seem like child's play.

## My Dark Night of the Soul ... Hookers (?)

About two months earlier, also on a Friday night, if memory serves me right, I became acquainted with a German girl by the name of Heidi. Sounds innocent enough, no? But don't be fooled! Don't make the easy error of picturing a barefoot, benevolent lass frolicking in the Alps. Instead, think Irma Grese. Think Nazism. Think of the worst that's rolled off Germany's schizophrenic assembly line. Picture, if you will, a big-boned blonde with mad, fanatical eyes and Jägermeister dripping from her chin, because it was precisely this manner of creature that descended on me and, with very little by way of preamble, ordered me to go home with her.

Obviously, I had my reservations—there was patently something wrong with the girl, but I also thought she'd be down for anal, which I happened to be curious about at the time. Accordingly, I shrugged my shoulders and told her to lead the way.

When we reached her place, she behaved not unlike how most women do in my presence: like helpless animals. To paint the picture more vividly, she struck at the seat of my pants like a desperate lioness at the ass of a gazelle and yanked and yanked to get it down.

I'd be lying if I said this didn't turn me on—it did—so, in keeping with the tone of events, I drove her face-first onto the bed and, after hastily slipping on a condom, gave it to her from behind with the vigor of a caveman. In the vagina, I should probably add. The anal, I imagined, was yet to come.

As it turned out, it wouldn't, because, well, there's no easy way of saying this, not even twenty seconds later, I was on the verge of spurting. An incredible turn of events, really, because, well, not only had this never happened to me before—or since, I might add—but, as a rule, I tended to punch at the other end of the spectrum, meaning girls only ever complained about my endurance to the extent that it chafed them. I kid you not. Sometimes they *begged* me to stop, too hurt to continue. Casualties of a sexual war, bloodied by a relentless, indefatigable machine-gun fire of 10-inch rounds.

On this night, however, for whatever inexplicable reason, the tide came in early, and it sent me into a real tizzy. I mean, I might not have liked this girl very much, but I sure as hell didn't want her to think of me as a quick shot. Who knew who she might tell? Charlie Jett became known as "The One-Minute Steak" after a girl tattled on him. I wouldn't have it.

Incredibly, in the nick of time, it occurred to me that if I were to cum very silently, fill my balloon without a grunt or a peep, then perhaps, just perhaps, this mishap might escape her notice.

I proceeded accordingly, and it went down without a hitch. When I started to spew, I not only remained as quiet as a mouse but also took great care not to ease up on the throttle, as lesser men are apt to do at this point.

From what I could tell, she was none the wiser.

Then, as the heavenly mists cleared from my eyes, an escape route appeared: I reduced my pumps to just under 180 per minute—to impart the idea that a measure of doubt had crept into my mind—and moments later, fell out of her with a loud moan.

"Nooo! Nooo!" I wailed. "I can't do it. I can't. I can't do it."

"You can't do what?" came the confused voice from behind me.

"I can't do it. I can't, I can't. I have ... a guurlfriend."

She tried her best to convince me that it didn't matter, but it was to no avail. I pulled up my pants and, after making sure I had all of my belongings, left.

Now, two months later, having not seen this girl

since, I found her huffing and puffing next to me like a wounded buffalo—a thing to be wary of, if you're unfamiliar with the psychology of wounded buffaloes.

Thinking that I should strike a friendly note, I opened negotiations with a "Hey, you! How are—"

"Is that her?" she cut in, glaring at Yvonne. "Is that the girlfriend?"

"Uh—oh—oh no," I said, remembering that I was supposed to have a girlfriend. "No, we,"—I turned my voice down and drew closer, hoping to keep Yvonne out of the loop—"we broke up last week."

She snorted violently, blasting me back by a foot.

"Do you really think I *believed* that story? Do you really think I *fell* for it?"

"I—I don't know. You don't have to believe it. But that's the truth."

She shook her head.

"I knew something was off. I just knew it."

"I don't really know what to say."

She jumped up.

"I just came here to tell you that. I couldn't help myself. I'm going now."

She stomped off.

"Jeepers," I said, turning back to Yvonne. Much to my relief, she seemed to be taking the thing in her stride.

"Who was that?" she asked eagerly.

"Just some girl," I said, feathering my fingers down her jaw. "She's struggling to get over me." And before she could probe the matter further, I plugged her lips. She made a few half-hearted mumbling sounds but quieted down soon enough.

Peace and prosperity would not be ours for long. Not even a minute later, the angelic sound of a female chant reached my ears. I extricated my face from her freshly washed hair to investigate.

Much to my surprise and delight, the girls were … *looking at me! chanting at me! smiling at me!* I couldn't quite decipher the words—the band had just hit the chorus of "Sweet Caroline"—but to show them that I was a fun guy and open to group sex, I cracked a dazzling smile and mouthed along.

I also mirrored their chosen gesticulation: a raised pinkie.

The scene rapidly dissolved into a hellish nightmare when, moments later, I realized the girl on the far left was Heidi. The words of the chant suddenly became clear: "Small *peeeenis!* Small *peeeenis!* Small *peeeenis!*"

Dear readers, I was just about to get up and extract Caesar Augustus when it dawned on me that Yvonne might not yet have deciphered this slander. If so, she'd still be looking favorably upon me—perhaps even more so now, with so many women seemingly having the hots

15

for me.

So, I played it cool. I stuck to the status quo: kept mouthing, kept smiling, kept pinkying. I kept it all up until the ensemble had bundled through the door and up to the piano lounge in a fit of giggles. Then I turned back to her, shaking my head with a shy, modest smile— the look of a man slightly embarrassed by his own magnetism.

She wasn't having any of it. She slapped my arm and said, "Okay, tell me now! Who's that girl? And what did you do to her?"

"I didn't do anything to her!"

"*She* didn't seem to think so."

"As I told you, she's struggling to get over me. We hooked up once, and now she's acting all crazy."

"Hmm …"

"What?"

"How often do you do this?"

"What?"

"Hook up with girls."

I chuckled.

"Not often."

"You do! You're such a liar!"

"No, really, I don't."

"Yeah, yeah …"

"Kiss me," I said, leaning in. She pushed me away.

"No! I barely know you."

"Get to know me, then!" I opened my arms like Jesus. "I'm an open book."

She sat up excitedly.

"Okay, tell me about your talents."

"My talents? Ah, well, let me see now." I slumped forward like Rodin's *The Thinker*. I sat like this for a few seconds, pondering her question, then sighed and straightened. "My only talent, I regret to say, is false modesty."

She nearly spat out her drink.

"Hold it in, lady!" I said, rubbing her back.

She took a few seconds to contain herself, then said, "But didn't you say you're a writer? I recall you saying something like that." And as she said it, a feverish, hungry light flared in her eyes. The implication was clear: she had the hots for writers.

Feeling not a little chuffed, then, I said, "Yeah, that's right."

"Impressive."

Shrugging sluggishly, like a sunbathing dog after being asked who's a good boy, I said, "Ah, you know, what can I say?"

"What do you write about?"

"Cricket, mainly."

"Cricket?" She looked confused. Then the light of understanding went on and, to my stark horror, girlish amusement entered her features. "The *sport?*"

I flinched. She had pronounced "sport" like a squeaky toy.

"Yes," I muttered, eyeing her resentfully, "but I'm also working on other stuff—more serious stuff—on the side. The cricket is just to pay the bills, really."

"So you want to be a serious writer?"

"What do you mean do I 'want' to be a serious writer?!" I blasted out. "I *am* a serious writer! Cricket is Big Business!"

"Okay," she said, taken aback. "And what did you study? Journalism or …?"

"Why do you just assume I studied something? Why did I have to study something?"

"So … you didn't study something?"

"No, but believe you me, I've paid my dues! I've done my homework!"

"Okay."

"I have!"

And then she burst out, "I believe you! Jeez."

A little rattled by her response, I turned my vehemence down a notch and just said, "Hmm, okay."

But it seemed as if I would now be up against it because she turned away to look at the band in the distance and seemed out of it all of a sudden. This only intensified my fear and, you know how it is when you're chatting to a bird you want to have your way with but she's not paying any attention to you—you tend to keep chatting. A fatal instinct.

"In any case," I added hastily, "it was a choice. I didn't want to be boxed in by the authorities. I mean, look at how they terrorize professors. Can you imagine how they treat fellow *students?*" I waited for the laugh—I mean, I thought it was good stuff—but didn't even get so much as a chuckle. So I plowed on: "And remember! Some of the best writers never went to university: George Orwell, Mark Twain, Shakespeare. They—"

As if the deplorable reputation of third wheels couldn't get any worse, her friend chose that very moment to materialize next to our booth like a fucking leprechaun.

Yvonne got out to confer with her. The friend prattled a bit, Yvonne gave the nod, then came back to me and said, "I have to go."

I sat up like a meerkat.

"What? Why?"

"Annette's not feeling well."

"But—"

"I'm sorry! I'll see you around."

And then she left. Just like that.

"Fuck!" I slammed my fist down. "Fuck! Fuck! Fuck!"

I was furious, absolutely fucking furious. Passers-by

eyed me with apprehension; I glared at them in turn. I stewed in this venomous hate for quite some time, cursing under and over my breath, taking messy sips of beer. But then, you know, there comes a time in life when you're presented with a choice: to be a victim and take up a life of video games and misogyny, or to be a victor.

To do the latter, you can't merely blame the woman and her accomplice, no matter how objectively rotten their behavior. You also need to take stock of your own actions—or lack thereof. And because I am a man of no ordinary caliber, it took me little time to realize that most of the blame for this painful defeat rested squarely on my broad, muscular shoulders. It was my failure to have written something of note that was the crux of the matter.

If I had been able to tell Yvonne that, instead of arcane articles about Jacques Kallis and Sachin Tendulkar, I authored novels and plays about the most pressing social issues of our time—one of which, perhaps, had won a Pulitzer Prize and was now being adapted into a major motion picture starring Leonardo DiCaprio, Natalie Portman, and a withering Al Pacino—she would've reacted less like Lolita in one of her funny moods and more like a star-struck groupie. When her friend surfaced, moaning about wanting to go home, she would've told her to get a fucking cab.

Now, this wasn't the first time I had lamented my failure to have written something "serious". There had been many a night when, sitting in a dump like Crazy Joe's, I thought to myself, boy oh boy, you're wasting your time here. You should be at home, working on a play or a novel—or even a work of non-fiction, provided it was about matters of life and death and not some Mickey Mouse topic. But never before had I been so disgusted with myself that I felt like smashing a beer bottle into my forehead. And it's because, until now, my failure to act hadn't really cost me. The worst I ever got was a funny look. But it never became a thing—and I always, *always* still managed to bring home the gravy.

Tonight, I spilt it.

This rage fired me up like never before. Suddenly, huffing and puffing like Heidi earlier, I was raring to go, ready to put in the work. And thanks to a former half-arsed attempt, I already had a topic in mind: hookers.

Crazy Joe's was packed with them—I could see four just from my perch—and it once dawned on me that a sincere, compassionate tale about these ladies would be just the kind of thing to shower me with the literary prestige I was after.

Unfortunately, I didn't know enough about them to just start scribbling away like a prophet. First, I would have to do some research. Approach them and have a little chat. All I really knew was that they hailed from Kalashnikov countries like the DRC and were usually patronized by white foreigners out for a bit of fun before flying back home to the wifey.

Other than this, I knew zilch, didn't know what varieties of shit went down after they left CJ's, once these boys had gained the freedom of privacy, but I intended to find out.

Two danced with Aussies, another laughed at the solicitations of an elderly buzzard, and the fourth scanned the dance floor.

I drew a bead on the latter.

I downed the last of my beer, then suavely walked over and slotted in next to her. Following a moment of tactful silence—of the essence on these occasions—I tilted my head towards her and said, "You're a hooker, right?"

Silence.

"Excuse me?"

"A hooker." I turned towards her. Then I frowned, for I had expected to see some relief—sexual arousal, even. I mean, compared to the usual iguanas that approached her, I was Don Juan.* And yet, for whatever reason, she was beholding me as if I had kicked her cat. All horror and shock.

---

* Some say I resemble a young Vincent Cassel. I can't say I disagree.

"No. I'm. Not."

You can imagine my confusion. I mean, what? What the fuck was she on about? Why would she say that? But then it struck me—she must think I'm a cop! After all, I was nearly half the age of her usual prospect. Obviously, she would be suspicious. So, to put her mind at ease, I patted her arm and said, "Don't worry, I'm not a cop. I'm a writer. I'm on *your* side."

"But I'm not a hooker!"

I winked at her.

"Yes, you are."

She reached behind her and grabbed hold of her comrade. The comrade promptly appeared.

"This guy thinks I'm a hooker!"

The comrade, who had been eyeing me suspiciously from the outset, blew up, giving her the aspect of an angry drill sergeant.

"What!" She got up in my face. "Are you telling me that when you see a young, beautiful black woman in a tight dress,"—she motioned towards her friend—"you just automatically assume she's a *hooker?*"

I gasped.

"Of course not! It's just that I've been coming here for years, and I see you guys—"

"Guys!"

"Sorry, my bad." I raised my hand in apology. "I

meant ladi—"

"You think I'm a hooker *as well?*"

This tipped me over the edge.

"Of course I do! Can't you just be honest with me? I'm not here to do you in; I'm here to help you. I want to write a story about you, about what you go through, about what these tourists do to you. I want prostitution to be *legalized*. I want to be your voice!"

Just as I was getting on a roll, the friend burst into tears and rushed toward the exit. The comrade, after taking a moment to retrieve her jaw from the floor, set off in pursuit. The old man also joined the chase, but not before throwing his arms up and shouting, "What did you do?"

I swiped the air dismissively, then signaled the bartender.

"A Cape Dutch!"

I looked around in disgust. The other whores—or non-whores—were now being squeezed into a sandwich by the Aussies. Through the window, a street boy looked on, transfixed. Next to him, his friend eyed a beautiful woman at a table by the stage, mouthing "I love you" repeatedly, steaming up the glass. She teased him with a smile while digging her nails into her lover's leg under the table.

Everybody else, except for a few loners having dark

thoughts in dark corners, was on their feet, swaying, dancing, drinking, singing, sweating, flirting, smoking, groping, chatting, pushing, forgetting—I felt a tap on my forearm. My pint was sputtering on the counter.

I paid and downed a third of it. When the opening stanza of "Don't Stop Believin'" made me want to fling the other two-thirds at the vocalist, I made my way back to the adjoining room. How quickly things can change, I pondered sadly as I passed through, eyeing the now-empty booth in which Yvonne had groped me so keenly. Would I see her again?

It was with a lump in my throat that I trudged up the creaky staircase to the piano lounge. Reaching the top, I vaguely hoped I wouldn't run into Heidi and her ensemble. All I wanted now was a bit of peace, some time to reflect, and based on my previous interaction with these savages, they were sure to prevent that.

Mercifully, Lady Fortuna spared me the ordeal. There were only a dozen or so patrons in the dimly-lit room, all of the quiet, non-chanting sort by the looks of it. It didn't surprise me, either. The pianist was playing a very slow, very gloomy melody—appropriate for my mood, but hardly the kind of tune to keep a girl like Heidi spellbound.

I collapsed onto a stool by the bar and buried my face in my hands. Fucking hell. This life. How would it all end?

After a few more sombre moments, I swiveled around to get a proper look at the pianist.

I squinted. Could it be? Could it really be him?

## Fellatio (?) ... Laurence Chalmers, BSc (Psych)

A few months earlier, because I'm a refined sort of chap, I took a lady to a concert at the City Hall.

We arrived early, and so had enough time for a glass of wine in the foyer. We also, well, rather I—at her insistence—bought one of those glossy booklets they have at these things. It was titled *Symphonic Spring: Rademeyer Plays Liszt*.

Rademeyer, we soon learned, was the surname of the soloist, Daniel: a young, up-and-coming pianist who had won multiple major international competitions and was now making his professional debut with the Cape Town Philharmonic Orchestra.

Next to his description was a picture: a twenty-something man with light-brown hair, blue eyes, and the symmetry of a manikin.

We were still examining his features when, lo and behold, the man appeared in the flesh! Came strolling past us in a black tux—the crowd parting for him as if he were Moses—smiling, waving, shaking hands, all in the manner of a man who imagined himself the star of a high-budget cologne advert.

It was sickening.

My date, on the other hand, seemed to be falling for all of this Dorian Gray shit, because, when he left the room, she turned to me and said, "Oh, wow, he's like … flawless."

Some hag next to us chipped in, "Isn't he? And so good. Such a friendly, well-mannered child. Wouldn't harm a fly. I've known him since he was a boy."

"Humph," was all I could say. I knew all too well what friendly, well-mannered boys were capable of. And my cynicism would bear out, because immediately there-after I headed to the restroom for a piddle and, upon entering, found this friendly, well-mannered boy in a position so weird, so unexpected, that a trickle of drool threatened to escape my mouth. I mean, there he was, in a cubicle—with the door as wide open as a teenager's heart—fondling his testicles while straining to fellate himself! Yes, fellate himself!

An arresting image, I think you would agree.

I didn't stop and buy popcorn, but my bulging eyes were glued to the scene for long enough to see him jolt and cover up. By the time I reached the urinals and settled into a perplexed stance, I heard him leave the cubicle and, rather surprisingly, but to his credit, stop at the basin to wash his filthy paws before exiting. My mind was racing: why didn't he just suck himself off in his green room? Why was he even on that side of the building to begin with? Why wasn't he warming up or something?

Initially, I thought that he might be some sort of an exhibitionist, but then I recalled that exhibitionists actually *want* to be seen, that the thought of some unsuspecting stranger goggling at their goods is the fountainhead of their zeal, and that this Rademeyer had been more redolent of Biblical Adam—shy, ashamed, and in the market for fig leaves—than one of those sixty-something European chaps who traumatize children at the beach.

I kept chewing the thing over. By the time I returned to my date, I had formed a more plausible hypothesis— one I chose not to divulge to keep her mind on more appetizing subjects.

Instead, I pushed the "auto-fellatio" narrative, which she found a hoot. In fact, I'd go so far as to say it helped me procure some of the good stuff later that evening; you know, by sort of planting the idea in her head.

But this is not of the essence. What's of the essence is that this new hypothesis was far more plausible than the one in which this pianist strained, at a most inopportune time and place—in a tux, no less—to fellate himself. And my theory only grew in plausibility thirty minutes later when he sat down to perform Liszt's *Piano Concerto No. 1*.

Sweating like Dick Nixon, he looked tight and nervous, a mere shadow of the confident, carefree figure that had strolled through the foyer. And despite hammering through the concerto's ferocious opening section agreeably, he consummately butchered the serene lines that were supposed to follow.

This in itself raised an eyebrow, but it was his response to this blunder more than anything that made me sit up and take notice. Instead of taking the prescribed deep breath and getting back on the horse, as it were, he snapped and, as one might expect from a man flung out of a rollercoaster, shouted, "Fuuuuuuuuuuuck!"

I don't know much about classical music and its historical happenings, but I imagine this was a highly unusual event. To his credit, he got a grip on himself and finished well, but for someone supposedly as competent as he was, that initial breakdown was telling.

I was so inspired by these events, I told my date I'd hunt him down and coax him into spilling the beans. I even got so far as to come up with a viable plan of action: introduce myself as a sympathetic Oxford-educated psychologist,* and under this guise break the awkward news of our restroom encounter, hoping that the nature of my profession would make it easier for him to open up to me. It was all very exciting.

But then the next day rolled around and, having had two very satisfying bites of the sexual carrot the previous evening, I no longer felt the drive. You know how it goes: you get laid, you get lazy.

So, I let the whole thing go, completely forgot about it—that is, until this Friday evening when, in a state of near-criminal ambition, I swiveled around and saw this very same Daniel awash in candlelight behind Crazy Joe's baby grand.

His appearance had a most marked effect on my mood. Perked me right up. Lady Fortuna sure knows how to slap you around, but she's also wise enough to rub your cheek from time to time and say "Come, come now" to keep you in the game. What electrified me even more was the fact that she had clearly slapped him around a bit as well.

Gone was the polished, elegant fellow who had floated through the City Hall. In his place sat a kind of scruffy bum: hair a mess, beard unshaved, and body stuffed into a shirt so crinkled it looked as if it had spent the previous night in a heap on the floor. He also had this dark,

* I grew up in Oxford.

31

somber, Sunday-afternoon air about him.

Two gloomy pieces later, he downed what was left of his drink and made his way over to the only other patrons at the bar: a mid-to-late-twenties couple a few stools to my right.

I got the distinct sense I knew the fellow from somewhere. He was a big, neat, together-looking chap—of the benign, whole-grain sort that parents are only too happy to see their daughters drag through the front door. Not my sort, then, and yet we must've mingled at some point.

His darling, on the other hand, was very much my kind of company: a fun-sized blonde with the toned, sun-kissed physique of a feisty little tennis player. Sadly, she didn't evoke any sense of familiarity.

The chap stood up and, smiling warmly, shook hands with Daniel.

"Well played, bud," he said. "I really enjoyed that."

"Thanks, Pierre." Daniel placed his empty glass on the counter. "Another one, please, Charles," he said to the bartender.

The keep reached for a bottle.

"Yeah," started the woman tepidly, as if restraining a more honest impulse, "it was nice—"

"But?"

Her response was blunt. "It was depressing. I'm not

surprised they want you gone."

Daniel shrugged. "I don't care."

"Children rarely do." She hopped off her stool. "We're meeting friends across the road. You coming?"

The bartender slid Daniel his whisky. He raised it in a mock toast.

"I think I'm good here."

"Of course you are." She turned to Pierre. "I'm going to the bathroom, then we must go."

Once she was gone, he got up and joined Daniel by the counter. Like the former, he propped himself up on an elbow and gazed at the piano in the distance. Reeking of an agenda, he said, "So, how have you been, bud?"

"Okay," said the other listlessly.

The big man seemed a bit deflated. "I see, I see." He turned his gaze to the floor. Having frowned at it for a while, he said, "And, eh, have you heard from Layla again?"

Daniel's glass halted just short of his lips. Eventually, through what may or may not have been gritted teeth, he said, "No."

"Nothing?"

"Only saw her housemate earlier ... while I was playing."

"Her housemate?"

"Some girl. Can't remember her name."

Pierre turned to him.

"Why don't you just give her a call, bud? I know you think—"

Daniel swung around.

"I don't just think, Pierre. I know, I *know* I'm not good enough for her."

Pierre sighed and turned away. So did Daniel. Then the former said, "I think I've told you this before. Not long before I met your sister, I felt a bit … I felt a bit as I think you do now, and then—"

"Pierre, please don't start with this again. I've told you already, I'm not interested. I already joined you—"

"You were hungover! You didn't experience it properly. You need to give it time. Trust me. He can help you. He can save you. You need Him, Daniel. You're in pain. You need something to hold on to. I can see it. You don't like to talk about it, but it's clear. I'm worried about you, bud. Ella is worried about you. Please, think about it. I can help you—the Lord can help you."

"Look," said Daniel, showing all the signs of a cork that's about to pop, "I know all of this is coming from a good place. I know you *mean* well, but I'm just not interested. And I'm fine. Not at my best, but fine."

"You're not fine. Please, bud, let me help you."

Daniel didn't answer. He was looking past him at the lassie approaching, her face flushed with anger. "Somebody puked in the bathroom. It's disgusting!"

Daniel smirked. "Well, at least you don't have piss all over your floor."

"How would *you* know?"

Daniel chuckled.

She turned to Pierre and said, "Come."

Pierre gave Daniel a friendly punch on the shoulder and said, "See you later, bud."

"Yeah," replied the other, draining the rest of his whisky. "Another one, Charles."

"Sure, Daniel."

Poor sod. He had no idea what was coming his way. As all of this was going on, I recalled the plan I alluded to earlier, of my assuming the role of an Oxford-educated psychologist to help win him over, and decided to shove it into action. As a seasoned actor who had assumed several significant roles in primary school, this wangle was right up my alley.

Accordingly, it was with an easy, self-assured manner that Laurence Chalmers, BSc (Psych), hopped off his stool and, having switched on his phone's voice recorder, moved in.

Slotting in next to the lad, I said, "Evening, old boy. Sorry to disturb you like this. I'm just a little curious: what's the surname of that big fellow you just spoke to? I'm convinced I know him from somewhere."

He turned his head and, clearly in no mood for mysteries, said, "Le Roux."

I rubbed my chin thoughtfully. "Le Roux, Le Roux … No, I'm at a loss, but I'm sure it will come to me."

His whisky arrived.

"Thanks, Charles."

I waited for him to take a sip and then said, "So, you're bidding this place goodbye then, eh?"

He turned to me and said, "How do you know that?"

I chuckled.

"Well, that bird who was here just now said something to the effect. I didn't mean to eavesdrop, old boy, but her voice carries. Well-suited to shepherding."

A puff of amused air escaped his nostrils. "True."

I took a cool, long draught of my beer. Bullshitting makes you thirsty.

"By the way," I said, "you were excellent tonight."

"Thanks."

"I especially liked that, what was it—the third-to-last piece you played?"

"Gershwin's second prelude."

"Yes, that's the one! Just fantastic." I took another stab at the beer and felt a surge of excitement. "That said, I think you have an even better feel for Liszt."

I had expected animation, and animation was what I got. He started as if I had poked him with a bradawl.

"Liszt! When did you hear me play Liszt?"

"Last year. In the City Hall."

He goggled at me.

"Are you kidding me? That was a fucking train wreck!"

"Oh, come now, it wasn't that bad. Yes, you had the little blunder at the onset, but the recovery was quite admirable. That's what matters. Don't you recall what Rocky Balboa said? 'It ain't about how hard you're hit. It's about—'"

"Stop. Please just stop."

"Okay," I said, shrugging. "I do not wish to aggravate you. In fact, old boy, I'm here to help you." I leaned in and lowered my voice. "To do so, however, I must first break some news which, in the short run at least, might perturb you somewhat."

I could see his hand tightening on his glass.

"Prior to that concert," I continued, feeling the rising anticipation of a chap who is about to detonate a bomb, "I found you in a … how shall I put this … in a somewhat compromising position."

I don't know if you've ever seen a deer get a whiff of gun oil, but essentially what happens is this: they freeze, their eyes grow wide with fear, and the tuft of grass which had been churning merrily in the corner of their mouth suddenly comes to a halt. Daniel very nearly matched this description in the wake of my statement.

"What do you mean?" he said in a sort of faltering, gulping way.

"Well, let's put it this way," I said, calm as chamomile, "I could've entered the restroom at a somewhat less revealing moment."

His face drained of color.

"It was *you!* You were the one who walked in on me!"

"That's correct, sir."

"What exactly did you see?"

I glanced at the bartender, then leaned closer. "I saw it all, bud. Everything. The whole shebang. In detail."

He buried his face in his hands.

"But don't be embarrassed about it," I said, rubbing his back. "Really, I don't judge. These kinds of things happen."

He suddenly looked up, his bright blue eyes saturated with moist desperation. "Have you told anybody?"

Smiling like a doting father at his frightened son, I squeezed his shoulder and said, "Not a soul, old boy, not a soul. Your secret is safe with me."

"Really?"

Tears of gratitude threatened to break free.

"Really."

"But—why? Most people would—"

"Run with that story like a dog with an itch? I know.

It's regrettable. But I'm not like them. I don't spread smut. I'm a psychologist. I aim to understand, not undermine."

"I … really appreciate that. Sorry—what's your name?"

"Chalmers, Laurence Chalmers."

## The Disease That Must Not Be Named

And so we became amigos. We smiled, we shook hands. He hailed the barkeep and ordered whiskies. He asked me to tell him more about myself. I did so, too. Told him about my formative years at Magdalen College when I first started pondering the nature of man—Is he good? Is he bad? Is he something in between? I missed those years, I told him.

Then, when we received our drinks, and as that initial glow of pleasant emotion that accompanies a fake new friendship began to diminish, I returned the conversation to more commercially viable topics.

"Old boy, tell me something, if you don't mind. That night—why didn't you just close the door?"

He smiled wryly and was just starting to reply when I interrupted him, a neat idea having come to mind.

"Sorry to cut you short like that, but"—I slyly motioned toward the bartender—"wouldn't you rather we

40

move over there?" I pointed at a snug, isolated couch at the back of the room.

If the man hadn't been convinced of my honest-to-god goodness before this show of consideration, he most certainly was now. A strange, mellow light entered his eyes, and he shook his head ever so slightly, as if to say, "Gosh, how wrong I had been about you."

"Yes, let's do that."

Having relocated to the aforementioned couch and wiggled ourselves comfortable, I said, "So, where were we? Ah, yes! The door. Why didn't you just close it?"

"I did, but I couldn't see a thing. So I opened it a touch to get more light."

"I see, I see, interesting, but I recall the gap being wide enough to shed light on—and excuse my vulgarity—more or less ten cocks?"

He found my remark mildly funny.

"I know. It swung open as I bent over and I … I guess I thought I'd be quick, so I left it."

"Why didn't you just leg it to your green room? I mean, the concert was about to begin. Why were you even on that side of the building to begin with?"

His eyes flashed with self-loathing.

"Because I'm a fucking narcissist, that's why."

I arched my eyebrows academically and said, "Let me be the judge of that, old boy."

"I'm telling you, I was there solely to get attention, to show my smug face in the foyer. The stopover in the restroom was nothing but a pretext."

"I actually remember you passing through. My date was so hot for your form, old boy, I think she would've gladly escorted you to the restroom."

He blushed. "Yes, well, luckily she didn't. It's difficult enough finding out you have an STD without having a girl in on the matter. And I doubt she would've been as understanding about it as you've been."

If I hadn't intended to juice Daniel right down to the pip, I would've leaned back at this point, lifted a lazy, aristocratic finger at the bartender, and asked him to bring me his finest Cuban cigar. Why? Because he had just confirmed my hypothesis. He had not, as I had initially suspected, tried to fellate himself. Instead, he had, as per my later, more thoughtful hypothesis, which I artfully withheld from you until now, been inspecting the rotten fruits of a venereal disease. What led me to this conclusion? Remembering how I once stood hunched over like that, fearing the worst.

"It's my job, old boy," I said humbly. "I'm supposed to be understanding."

"Still, I really appreciate it. And I'm sorry I had a go at you earlier. I'm just going through a rough patch."

Clasping his trapezius sympathetically, I said, "Don't

worry about it, don't worry about it one bit. And feel free to talk to me, okay? I don't mind lending an ear." I released the trap. "How about that luck though, eh? Of all the evenings ..."

"Well, I actually noticed something odd down there a few days earlier already while ..." He blushed again. "... shaving, but it caused me to arrive late for a rehearsal because I just couldn't stop looking at this thing. So I decided not to look down there again until after the concert—to stay focused. Well, obviously that didn't happen."

I nudged him.

"Like to look at your cock, eh? I like to contemplate my own when the opportunity arises. Very normal, that is ... the habit."

Missing the deeper element in my joke, he just smiled and said, "Yeah, but I was also beginning to think that it had probably just been a false alarm, that if I had a look now, I'd see that everything was fine, and I could put the issue to rest. So, on the night of the concert, I thought, ah, fuck it, and had a look."

"Did you immediately know what it was?"

"I was very confused about that. A few days earlier, there was just this one thing ... this papule; now, I could count at least a dozen of them, all in the same area. And then there was also one which was not only bigger than the others but also considerably redder. So I started thinking I might have multiple STDs. But which ones? I only knew four: syphilis, herpes, gonorrhea, and genital warts. But what did each entail? Warts seemed to explain itself pretty well, but wasn't herpes something similar? And which one oozed? Gonorrhea? Or was it syphilis? And didn't syphilis produce a sore of some kind? But what exactly was a sore? Was it supposed to hurt? And didn't you go *blind?* I decided on syphilis and herpes."

"Good god!"

"I wanted to weep, and was close to, but then I thought: could I really have *two* STDs? I mean, one … but two? It seemed like too much. So I bent over to have another look, and that's when you came in.

"I was in some state rushing out of there. And the whole way back to the green room, people are coming up to me—wanting to talk, wishing me good luck. But that actually helped me get my head straight. Seeing them all reminded me how much worse the evening could get if I didn't get my shit together. So I went through my routine and felt pretty focused by the time I stepped onstage.

"But then, as I'm receiving the crowd's applause, I spotted, maybe three rows from the front, this bearded man … looking amused. Didn't applaud. Just sat there, looking up at me, smiling. I thought it was you. I thought it was the guy who had walked in on me—and it fucked me completely.

"Somehow I got through the opening without problem, but then my thoughts started running away with me: was that a whisper? Was he telling the people next to him what he saw? Were they telling the people next to them? Were they all laughing at me? I could feel myself slipping, tightening. And then—" He sighed. "I couldn't believe what I had done. I had never done anything like it. I also didn't think I could do anything worse, so the rest came easy—it didn't matter."

I slapped his thigh.

"As I've told you already, old boy, I thought you were splendid, regardless of that little mishap. But, tell me now, what did you end up having?" I pointed south.

"The next day, I saw a doctor in Bellville—"

"Bellville?" I was confused. Bellville was about half an hour's drive away. "Couldn't you get an appointment in town? Or do you live there?"

"No, I just … I guess I was afraid a doctor in town might recognize me and talk out, so I wanted to be safe."

I eyed him sternly.

"A breach of doctor-patient confidentiality is a serious offense, old boy."

"I know, but I wanted to be sure, and this guy seemed like my best bet. In any case, he told me that these 'growths'"—he made air quotes—"were caused by something called HPV—short for human papillomavirus.

"He said it's one of the less serious STDs—for men, at least; women can get cervical cancer—because its symptoms are all superficial. He also told me it's very common and that it usually remains dormant. Most people never even find out they have it.

"All of this obviously made me feel much better, but as he's freezing these 'growths'"—he once again made air quotes—"with liquid nitrogen, I became bothered by the fact that he was also referring to them as 'growths', despite giving off the impression that it wasn't the correct term. So, I pressed him about it and, after beating around the bush for a bit, he admitted that, in fact, they were genital warts."

"No!" I said, pseudo-horrified. "The fucker!"

"And that wasn't the end of it! Two weeks later, by which time I was supposed to have healed, I was no better. The 'warts'," he said, and again made air quotes, "remained."

Wanting to get to the bottom of all this air-quoting, I parroted the gesture and said, "The 'warts'?"

He just smiled and said, "Just wait, you'll see. So, two weeks later, I went back to this doctor, and this time he gave me some cream. The reaction this thing had on me … shit. Everything went all red and started swelling up.

I immediately went online to read up about it, and it said it might never go away—*might never go away!* Can you imagine?

"On the same site, I found out what else the good doctor had kept from me: that HPV can't be cured, that even if the warts were to disappear completely, they could come back at any time. Jesus, what a nightmare.

"To top it all off, a girl I had been seeing showed up at my house that afternoon, high as a kite, wondering why she hadn't heard from me for a while. I tried my best to get her away, but she pushed past me into the house and started going wild on my carpet, begging for it. I couldn't resist her, man. That whole morning, I had been despairing about my sex life and how it would never be the same again, then she comes along, begging for it.

"I became, I became … quite aggressive with her—but I didn't expose her to anything! I just got her off and then … got myself off in the bathroom."

Remembering the name of the girl Pierre mentioned earlier, I said, "Was that Layla?" And seeing him frown, I said, "It's not just your sister's voice that carries, old boy."

He smiled and said, "No, Layla and I only met a bit later on … on Lion's Head one afternoon. I wasn't doing well at the time. I rarely went out of the house, spent most of my time in bed, didn't practice—even though

I had a big competition coming up. Going up there was the only thing that gave me any sort of joy.

"It gave me some perspective, being up there, in the wind and sun, with not so many women around." He went quiet. "And then I ran into Layla. I guess not so much ran into her as approached her. I knew it was a bad idea, that it could only end badly, but I couldn't help myself. There was something about her ... about the way she sat there, clasping her knees, looking out over the ocean. Something pure, something innocent, which made it even worse. But there it was.

"We hit it off from the start. She was so different from the girls I knew—mature, thoughtful, sensitive. She had just arrived from New York, here to volunteer as a dance instructor.

"We met up for dinner that evening, and it went really well. So well, in fact, that we made out. Obviously, I couldn't take things further, so I just got her a cab and headed home.

"The fucked up thing was: she was so *impressed* by this. She didn't say it, but I could see it in her eyes. For not pushing things, she thought I was the real deal, a gentleman. And this impression only grew stronger as time went by, because we started seeing each other a lot after that, got really close, and still all I ever tried to do was kiss her. Eventually, it got to the point where *she* tried to take things further.

"One night we were lying in bed, relaxing, when her housemate brought someone home, and we heard them having sex. At first, we just laughed about it, but then she started getting a bit turned on and feeling me up. And I was close to letting it play out, because I was nearly healed by then.

"After our first date, I was so desperate to get better, I made an appointment with a well-known dermatologist in town. And do you know what he told me? That the other doctor had fucked up. He had misdiagnosed me. I didn't have genital warts; I actually had a completely harmless disease called molluscum … something."

"What!"

I was shocked. I'd been operating under the high drama of genital warts, only to find out he had but a minor skin condition. It felt like a demotion.

"So you didn't even have an STD?" I asked in a kind of pleading way.

"No, I did," he said, much to my relief, "but it was a harmless one. And by pure dint of luck, that doctor had given me the correct cream for it. But the dermo reckoned that by pricking the papules, I'd heal more quickly. And so it happened. By that evening when we heard the housemate, I was basically fine. But the dermo had not yet given me the go-ahead, so, as difficult as it was to do, I pushed her away, saying there's no rush and I don't want her to think I'm just in it for sex and shit like that. Just floundering, really.

"Fortunately, her housemate burst into the room butt-naked moments later, upset about something the guy had done, which gave me an out. And two days later, the dermo cleared me!

"Jesus man, I was so happy, so happy … I could already see myself pitching up at Layla's that evening and, you know …" The light went out of his face. "But then, thanks to just one question, everything changed.

"As I was about to leave, he said he hoped he wouldn't have to see me again soon. I laughed and said it was unlikely, as I had met this really nice, decent girl. He said that reminded him of something.

"He explained that, while the STD I had contracted wasn't serious, it was an STD nonetheless, meaning I may have contracted other, more serious diseases which may not become apparent for years. In light of this—especially now that I've met this nice, decent girl—wouldn't I want to get tested for HIV? It'll only take a few minutes, and my medical aid would cover it." He shuddered. "The idea of getting tested had always terrified me, but never before had someone actually confronted me about it—and in a hospital, no less. It was too much. So I just said, 'No, that's fine,' and left."

You know, it just occurred to me that, by the time you read this, HIV might no longer be a thing. I mean, I don't want to blow my own horn here, but I'm unusually robust. Barring some freak accident, I'm bound to remain upright for many more years, during which time scientists might eradicate this little asshole. And it might lead you to wonder what all the fuss was about. Let me tell you.

HIV, at the time of writing, has no cure. It will cut you down unless, at some point, but ideally as early as possible, you get on antiretroviral drugs. Here's the thing, though, the all-important thing: in most cases, you may not experience any serious symptoms for *up to a decade.*

Conceivably, then, you could become infected and, as long as you don't get tested, pay no price for years, go on as per normal: sow your seed, get into relationships, get married, make babies, and have no legal obligation to tell anybody anything.

Get tested early, however, and wave goodbye to life as you know it. Now you *know* you have a deadly disease, and that makes all the difference. Infect someone now, and society will no longer merely think it's tragic. They'll also think it's criminal. They'll think *you're* a criminal. Infect someone now, and there will no longer be that gray uncertainty, helped along by years of dormancy and other sexual partners, about where they got it from. The finger of blame will point straight at you.

Accordingly, a chap with any sense (or decency, if he is so inclined) will think twice before sleeping around. He'll stay in on Friday evenings and read a book—or perhaps jump off a roof.

It's a fucking disaster! An evolutionary death blow! The only upside of getting tested early is that you may extend your life by a few years. But who gives a fuck about a few extra years if they'll be miserable? And nothing seems quite as miserable and pointless to a young man of sexual means as the prospect of forced celibacy, which a positive diagnosis would more or less amount to. At least, that's what most fuckboys *believe* it amounts to, whether it's the case or not—and that's all that matters.

Can you blame such a chap, then, when cordially invited to do the test, for saying, "Eh, no thanks, doc. I think I'll give it a skip."?

"He must've thought that I would just go ahead and sleep with Layla," Daniel continued. "But he was wrong. What he said made me realize that Layla was too innocent, too pure—not like the girls in the clubs and bars. Not like the girls in here." He gestured toward the bar area, where several women were congregated.

"She wasn't playing the same game as we were, so I

had no right to expose her to its risks. The choice was clear: I either had to get tested or leave her alone.

"It was all I could think about the rest of the day. I didn't know what to do. If I got tested and it was negative, I could be with Layla. But if it was positive? Then it was over. Not just with Layla but with everyone.

"If I chose not to get tested, on the other hand, I'd have to leave Layla, who I was in love with." Some very strong emotion suddenly rose up in him, giving him the appearance of an expanding balloon. "I mean, I was ready to risk my *life* for her!" he declared.

Unable to restrain myself, I winked at him and said, "Just not your sex life, eh, my boy?"

Just for a moment, he looked confused—narrowing his eyes, furrowing his brow—before he sort of collapsed in on himself and broke eye contact, ashamed.

I squeezed his trap and said, "But hey, don't feel bad about it, okay? I think it's commendable that you took such a strong, principled stance. Most lads wouldn't have given it a second thought." I removed my hand. "What did you end up doing?"

He took a moment to compose himself, then said, "That night, I met some Brazilian girl. I didn't try anything with her. I just wanted to be by myself, really, to think things through. But then she got touchy with me and, at one point, as I'm looking over her shoulder, I see this old man sitting by the bar, nursing his beer, and it dawned on me just how bad it must be for him, being surrounded by all these young people, reminding him of what he no longer had.

"Living with HIV, I realized, wouldn't be all that different, and I couldn't *stand* the idea. I was only twenty-three. I still had my best years ahead of me. Unlike him, women still wanted me. They were throwing themselves at me. Imagine having to say no to them all.

"I decided right then and there: fuck it, I wouldn't do the test."

He drained the rest of the whisky. "The next day, I ended things with Layla."

Hungry for details, I said, "How? What did you say?"

"First, I had to play in that competition I mentioned earlier and, well, that didn't exactly go according to plan."

"What happened?"

"We each had to play three pieces, and my first two went down without any issues. I was feeling pretty good. But then, during the last, this really difficult Scriabin étude, I suddenly started thinking about my blunder at the City Hall. I got tight and made a mistake. It wasn't even that bad. I could have easily recovered but, I don't know, in the moment, I just became so angry, *so* angry. That I could do this twice—I couldn't believe it. And I couldn't stand the idea of going on, of pretending that this level of play was acceptable to me. I wanted everyone to know just how high my standards were, just how much I thought of myself, so I smashed the keys and walked off.

"I met Layla outside and ended things right then and there. Said this thing between us was too distracting. That I was struggling to focus. That if I didn't get my shit together, my career would be over. She tried to convince me that we could work around it, spend less time together, whatever, but I just persisted. I hated myself for lying to her like that, hurting her like that—I still hate myself—but how could I have done otherwise? I simply didn't have it in me."

"Don't be so hard on yourself, old boy," I said. "Only the most honest people can admit they're liars."

He pulled out his phone and looked at the screen.

"Sorry, I need to take this." He placed it against his ear. "Hey, are you guys done? … Yes. Should I come over there or …? Okay, call me when you're outside … Yes, yes. Bye." He slid the phone back into his pocket. "My sister. They're heading home. Do you want to join us for a drink?"

"At your place?"

"Yeah, it's not far."

"Sure, why not."

I drained the last of my whisky and said, "But tell me,

now: what have you been up to since?"

"The breakup?"

"Yes."

"Drinking and fucking mostly. I also got this gig."

"I see … And Layla? Do you miss her?"

He turned toward the bar and made eye contact with a broad. She immediately smiled and waved in that quick, frantic way of one who had been staring. Daniel weakly returned the gesture.

"Sometimes I cry, I miss her so much," he said. "These girls"—he nodded in the direction of the goggler—"they mean nothing to me. It's only Layla I care about. If I could go back now, I'd take the test."

Stating what seemed like the obvious, I said, "So, why don't you?"

He frowned at me.

"Do you know how many girls I've been with over the past two months? Girls I barely knew? No, it'd be stupid. I'll just have to live with my decision."

I punched his shoulder.

"That's strong of you, my friend. That's real strong of you. A beautiful sacrifice."

An approaching pair of legs entered my field of vision. It was the girl from the bar.

"You have a visitor."

He looked up.

"Christ."

"Who is it?"

"A girl I hooked up with last weekend."

"Daniel!" the girl squealed.

"Alicia," he groaned.

She collapsed onto his lap, wrapping her arms around his neck.

"Why haven't I heard from you?" she sulked.

Casting me an apologetic look, he said, "Can you maybe—"

I jumped to my feet.

"Of course! Shall I meet you downstairs?"

"Yes, I'll be down in a minute. And Laurence—thank you. I appreciate it."

I winked at him.

"Don't mention it, old boy."

## The Girl Next Door ... A Daring Scheme

I floated away as if on a cloud. I could scarcely believe how quickly and to what extent my situation had looked up. Just a little while earlier, I was a picture of sorrow, at the lowest of lows, a shred of smudged cheese on the kitchen floor.

Now, through a stroke of good fortune and a dash of uncommon daring, I had gathered all the makings of a profound and serious story. Sure, I'd have to spin an ending, for Daniel's had tapered off rather dully, but that would be but a minor challenge for a writer of my timber. Yes, I would've been well satisfied if that had been the end of it. But it wasn't. Not even close. The table had merely been laid, and the entrée was about to be served.

I must say, she smelled terrific. No denying that. When I rounded the corner toward the stairs, and she came hurrying up to me, I only briefly appreciated her lissome, elegant features before I reeled from the sweet, succulent cloud of French perfume enveloping me.

"Hi, sorry to bother you," she said in a thin, tremulous American voice, eyes hazel and urgent, "but—can I ask you something?"

Sensing that the lassie was distressed, I snapped out of my daze and offered my most compassionate smile. "But of course!" I said. "What would you like to know?"

"Who's that girl sitting on Daniel's lap?"

I frowned, glanced back at the two, then turned to her and said, "You're not Layla, are you?"

"I am. How did you—did he say something about me?"

I couldn't contain my grin as I began to wonder what would happen, what searing explosions would go off in Daniel's fragile little brain, if he had to come around the corner at that very moment to see his psychologist, the man to whom he had just revealed his most intimate and embarrassing secrets, chewing the fat with the love of his life. This thought experiment turned out to be nothing but a starting point, however, a catalyst for my most daring scheme yet!

"He sure did," I said, practically licking my lips.

"What did he say?" she asked eagerly.

"Well, as his psychologist, I'm not at liberty to say, but I'll reveal this much: he is rather fond of you."

She got that dreamy look of a junkie soaking up a hit.

"He is?"

"He sure is alright."

Then her face hardened like crème brûlée.

"But only as a friend, right?"

"No! He really likes you, in the way that you *want* him to like you."

"Then why is he with that girl?"

"He's not with her. He's not with anybody. She just kind of collapsed onto him. He's actually trying to get rid of her."

"Oh … so he's still struggling with what happened at the competition? Is that why he's seeing you?"

"Unfortunately, yes," I said. "A tortured artist if ever there was one, really."

I glanced back to see how the two were getting along. Not too badly, as it turned out. The girl, now straddling him, seemed to have set herself the ambitious goal of sucking out all 32 of his teeth. She was going at it in a total-body way, too, curling her torso and hips like some oceanic creature from the deep. Thankfully, Layla was spared the ordeal. The wall blocked her view. Even so, I heard her emitting a long, miserable sigh. Turning back to her, I said, "You really miss him, don't you?"

She cast her eyes down.

"Yes."

"So let's get him back!"

She looked up hopefully.

"How?"

"We make him jealous!"

Her face fell. This was clearly not her idea of a red-hot plan.

"I don't know," she said. "I don't really like playing games."

"Games?—GAMES?!" I thundered. "Do you really think I play *games* with my clients? My paying clients? In case you don't know, I have a professional obligation towards them. I am bound by law not to play games with them."

"I know, I know. I didn't mean to question your integrity. It just sounded a bit odd." Then she added hastily, "So what do you have in mind?"

"Any moment now," I said, still sort of glaring at her, "he'll come downstairs looking for me. I suggest we head down to the dance floor and grind a bit. When he sees us, he'll get so jealous, he'll want you back immediately."

She wrinkled her nose as if I had suggested a trip to the local sewage plant.

"I don't know ..."

"Look, do you want him back or not? Because this is it. This is the only way. No amount of pleading or sweet-talking will do the job now. Only a strong emotion will. Jealousy will."

I straightened.

"Anyway, just tell me: are you in or out? He's coming any moment."

I glanced back at the two. Daniel was backing away from the couch as he gently removed the girl's hands from his shirt. I swung back to Layla and said, "He's coming! What do you say?"

She gave a quick nod. "Okay."

I grabbed her hand and started for the stairs. "We need to make sure the thing looks like one big coincidence," I said as we clattered down. "Let me do the talking. If he wants the lowdown, I'll tell him we met in a club one night and have seen each other a few times since. I'm Laurence, by the way."

The universe evidently wanted my plan to succeed. The band had vacated the stage, and instead of "Take Me Home, Country Roads" or some other sentimental rot, the ground floor was being pumped full of pornographic hip-hop.

"Splendid music for a bit of grinding, eh?" I said, ushering her toward the fray.

She smiled nervously.

I placed a hand on her shoulder. "It's going to be okay. Trust me."

I maneuvered her to face the region where Daniel would emerge and, after laying my hands on her hips, started rubbing up against her.

She went rigid.

"You need to relax!" I said. "We need to seem natural!"

She loosened slightly, but not enough, so I kept encouraging her: "That's better, but more, more ... Ah, yes, that's it ... shake it ... You're doing fantastic!" So fantastic, in fact, that I was getting an erection. "Ah, yes, yes ..." And then I spotted Daniel in the distance, his head sticking out above the crowd.

"He's coming!"

I bent Layla over with one arm while waving to catch Daniel's attention with the other. He quickly spotted me, flashed a grin, and made his way over. He laughed and shook his head when he saw what I was up to. I straightened Layla and hooked my arm around her waist.

Well, I don't think I've ever seen a man stop laughing and shaking his head more abruptly than Daniel in that moment. It had the flash-like quality of a sleight of hand.

"Daniel, old boy!" I said jovially. "I just ran into my squeeze. You wouldn't mind if she tagged along, would you? In fact, I've already kind of invited her ... Daniel?"

I should note that, as I hooked my arm around Layla's waist, one of the fellows next to us caught sight of my erection. Besides laughing his guts out about the sizable matter, he pointed it out to a friend. This commotion wasn't lost on Daniel, whose attention also shifted to the area of interest. His eyes widened. The next thing I knew, he grabbed me by the shirt and dragged me off through the crowd.

"Daniel!" I shouted, stumbling along like a tin can. "What the hell are you doing? Daniel!"

He slammed me up against a wall.

"You son of a bitch!" he hissed. "What kind of a sick game are you playing?"

"What the dickens are you on about?"

"You know what I'm on about!"

"No, I don't!" I pushed him away. "And I don't appreciate you manhandling me like this in front of my girl, especially not after everything I've done for you. What must she think of me now, eh?"

His certainty wavered. "But it's Layla! Layla!"

"Yes, Layla—and what about it?"

"My Layla!"

"Your Layla?"

"Yes! My Layla! From New York! We *just* spoke about her!"

"We did? When—" And then the penny supposedly dropped. I allowed a sunrise of comprehension to dawn across my features. "Oh my god!" I cried, throwing my hands to my face in a most convincing Edvard Munch.

"Yes!"

"I had no idea, old boy. Really, I had no idea."

"How? Same name? Same nationality?"

"I see what you mean," I said, looking real sorry, "and earlier, when you were talking about her, I considered the possibility. But the way you described her—it sounded so different from the Layla I know. I couldn't see the two being one and the same."

Fear crept up his skin like a snake.

"Different how?"

"Well, let me put it this way: I wouldn't describe her as 'pure' or 'innocent', if you know what I mean. She can't get enough of it, quite frankly."

He groaned and fell forward, bracing himself against the wall like a drunkard at the urinal. He turned to look at Layla, who sat at the edge of the dance floor with a sort of forlorn, what-has-it-come-to air.

"Are you together?"

"Nah, we just hook up."

He groaned another deep one.

"But listen," I said, "I know how much she means to you. So let's go back to your place, and the two of you can straighten things out. If she wants you back, I'll remove myself from the equation. How about that? Daniel?"

He straightened, looking ten years older. "Okay."

He led the way. When Layla saw us, she shot up like a startled duck. To set her mind at ease, I smiled encouragingly and gave her a secret thumbs-up. It didn't seem to help. She gave a quick, nervous step toward us and said, "Daniel! I had no idea! I promise."

To her shock, he hugged her.

"It's fine. How are you?"

"I'm okay. And you?"

"I'm … Are you joining us?"

"I think so," she said tentatively, looking at me for confirmation.

I was impressed. It was a thoughtful touch. It made our act more believable. I mean to say, it would've seemed rather callous had she just agreed on the spot with no thought for poor old Laurence, her present and aroused lover.

Fortunately for her and Daniel, Laurence Chalmers didn't only preach, he also applied. Stepping to the fore with my chin up, I said, "I have no objections. We are all adults here."

Layla's face brightened.

"Let's go," said Daniel. "My sister's waiting."

We spilled out onto the pavement, where said sister and her beefy beau awaited us. She pushed off from a colonnade and exclaimed, "Layla! What are you—" And then the words died on her lips. She had spotted my outstretched hand in front of her.

"Laurence," I said with Bond-like charm.

"He's a friend," said Daniel.

"Oh. Ella." She dropped my hand with insulting curtness and turned to Layla. "How have you been? Did Daniel tell you? Pierre and I are engaged!"

"What! Congratulations!"

She hugged Ella. I slapped Pierre on the back and said, "Hearty congratulations, old boy!"

"Thank you," he said, beaming.

We split into two parties: Daniel, Ella, and Pierre to one car, Layla and me to mine. Once out of earshot, Layla said, "Does Ella not know about you?"

"Meaning?"

"That Daniel is seeing a psychologist. Why did he say you're a friend?"

The possibility of Layla raising this issue had not escaped me, and, as befits a man of uncommon prescience, I had prepared a statement in advance.

"I'm glad you've brought this up. Unfortunately, as is the case with the majority of my male patients, he's ashamed to admit that he's vulnerable, that he needs help. He's afraid that society, especially you and his sister, will think he's weak. A sissy, if you will. I therefore implore you not to divulge your familiarity with this fact. He should be the one to inform you, once he's ready."

"I promise, I won't."

"Good."

I threw an arm over her shoulders.

"This is going well, though, eh? Did you see how he was looking at you? Fell in love with you all over again!"

She covered her smile with a hand.

"Just remember," I said, waving off a beggar, "we have to keep up appearances. Under no circumstances can he discover what we've been up to. If he does … well, well!"

## Desperate Scenes ... Irma Grese Returns

As you can imagine, I was a montage of conviviality and good humor behind the wheel. I chatted to Layla about this and that, and toward journey's end—as the fresh evening air streamed through the windows and cavorted with our hair—I whistled and swayed to Khachaturian's Masquerade Waltz.

But this musical mood received a considerable dent as I pulled up in front of Daniel's abode. I had imagined that, like most washed-up classical pianists, he would be lodging or occupying a friend's couch. Accordingly, when Layla told me to throw anchor in front of a three-story Victorian mansion erected about as high up on the slopes of Table Mountain as bricks are allowed to go, and informed me—while applying lip balm—that he lived there alone, I damn near crashed the car.

I mean, the kid was a veritable failure. How was such a thing possible? And I was just about to blurt out something to that effect when it occurred to me that Laurence Chalmers would already be familiar with such facts, so I held my tongue. Well, rather, I said, "Oh, nice."

My bladder once again announced itself with a sharp, insistent tug. I had been ignoring it for the past hour due to more pressing matters, but nothing pressed my matters more at present.

"Where's the nearest loo, old boy?" I asked Daniel as we came up the garden path. He was waiting for us on the porch.

"Down the hallway, last door on your right," he said, indicating behind him. "But my sister might be in there, so you—"

"Can't I just go on the lawn?"

"Sure."

So, as the lovebirds entered the house, I toddled back down the steps and lost sight of my ankles in what more closely resembled a lush meadow, desperately in need of one or two hungry cows, than a lawn.

I settled into a wide stance and, while admiring the full moon over Devil's Peak, shuddered near orgasmically as a thick, warm stream of urine gushed from my member, foaming and splashing over the blades of grass like Coca-Cola.

It was one of those eternal pisses. It seemed as if it would never end. It just kept coming and coming, as if from some magical spring. But all good things must come to an end, and what an end it was. As the final arc of golden liquid plunged to terra firma, I felt as if I was about two inches off the ground. Satori.

After shaking loose the last few drops, I felt so profoundly satisfied, I just stood there a while longer, taking it all in—sort of like Gatsby that one evening, when he gazed up at the stars. It's important to have these little moments, even in the midst of engineering a human drama. It settles you. But then you have to get back into it. Gatsby, for one, didn't acquire his fortune by urinating the whole time. So I zipped up and re-entered the fray.

The first form of life I encountered was Pierre, chilling solo in a drawing room of sorts. It was one of those rooms, often to be encountered in Victorian establishments, which seemed to be experiencing a kind of identity crisis—a cluttered repository of ottomans, Persian carpets, and settees, interspersed with heavy Dutch silverware, gilded Russian classics, obscure maps of the Levant, and, of course, a piano. There were even a few samurai swords mounted above the fireplace and, for a touch of the macabre, a taxidermal mishap staring down from a corner. It was as if Amerigo Vespucci or some such fellow had used the place as his personal dumping ground.

Crossing the threshold, I threw my arms up flamboyantly and said, "Pierre! How are you doing, my man? Have you seen the moon out there? A real doozy."

He rose from his chair and offered his hand.

"Laurence, right?"

I met his hand with a resounding smack.

"Right you are, old chap. Right you are. Tell me, where are the others?"

"Ella's gone to bed—she has a migraine. I think Daniel and Layla are in the kitchen."

"The kitchen, you say ... Well, let me go see what those two are up to. Kitchen at the back?"

"Yes."

The kitchen, it turned out, was unoccupied. The lights were on, Layla's intoxicating perfume lingered, but not a star-crossed lover met the eye. I frowned, and then I frowned no more, for I had spotted a slight opening in the sliding door leading to the backyard. I stole there and peered into the moonlit landscape. I spotted the two almost at once. They were about two big kudu jumps away, between a fountain and a tree, making out. Exceedingly romantic.

Stifling the cry of laughter that threatened to tear out of me, I pushed the door further apart and said, "Layla?"

The two broke apart.

"What, what are you doing?" I stuttered. "I thought,

I thought …"

With a shadow of perplexity trailing her words, she said, "I'm sorry, Laurence, but Daniel and I have a history. You and I … we weren't that serious. You knew that, right?"

"I guess so. It's just …" And then I sighed. "Never mind. I'm being selfish. You two belong together. I'll be on my way." I turned toward the door, took one step, then stopped and turned back. "Just one thing," I added.

"What?" said Daniel like a shot.

"You offered me a drink, old boy. Surely you won't send me off into the night without first soothing my aching heart, would you?"

"Of course not." He turned to Layla. "Wait for me upstairs? I won't be long."

"Okay."

In the hallway, I caught her in a lingering hug and said how much I'd valued our time together.

"Me too," she mumbled awkwardly before escaping upstairs.

"Sorry for the schmaltziness," I said as Daniel and I continued down the hall, "but I want her to remember me as someone who cared, you know?"

"I understand," he muttered.

We reached the drawing room just as Pierre came out. "I'm going to check on Ella," he said. "See you now."

"Whisky?"

"Yes."

We stepped into the room, and while Daniel drifted toward the drinks cabinet, I claimed a seat.

"How long have they been together?" I asked.

"Who?"

"Pierre and your sister."

"About a year."

"Not messing around, are they?"

He grinned.

"I think he is anxious for the honeymoon."

"You don't think they've …?"

"No," he said, handing me a glass. "He's too religious. He's building a church as we speak."

"A church?"

"Yeah, on their farm."

"How big?"

"Not sure. I still need to go look at the place."

I took a thoughtful sip and said, "So he's a farmer?"

"Winemaker. Bergschaduw?"

"I know Bergschaduw. I go to their wine festival every year. I'm actually surprised I haven't …" And then it dawned on me: I *had* seen him there! What's more, I had interacted with the man. We didn't talk much, but he hung out with our posse and, boy, did that turn into an evening.

"What?" said Daniel. "Laurence?"

My vision cleared.

"I just figured out where I know Pierre from."

"The festival?"

"Yes."

I hesitated.

"What?"

"I'm not sure I should tell you this."

"Jesus, just tell me."

"Okay, but remember: this was years ago, long before he hit it off with your sister, so don't judge him too harshly!"

"Just tell me!"

"Alright! So, I met him at this festival of theirs—he knew two of my friends—and we had just the most splendid time: drank wine, frolicked in the sun, danced—" I paused. I could hear Pierre's heavy footfalls coming down the stairs. "To make a long story short, we wound up at a rundown flat that evening where Pierre and a few lads took turns with a strung-out hooker. Not the first time, either, I believe. Seems as though he's turned over a new leaf, though, eh? Found Christ and all that. Pierre, you old dog!" I said when the devil breezed in. "Come and get your whisky!"

He sank into a chair and picked up his glass. We clinked—a sturdy, masculine sound—and then we turned to Daniel to complete the trinity. But the man didn't seem to be in a clinking mood. He rose and ambled over to the piano, where he stood gazing into the engine.

"I read an interesting article a while ago," he said pensively.

We waited for him to elaborate, to give us the gist, but got nothing.

Pierre and I exchanged a look.

"What was it about, old boy?" I ventured.

"A woman who got into a relationship with her doctor."

"A love story!" I exclaimed. "Let's have it."

He started to pace the room. "They met when he tested her for HIV." Out of the corner of my eye, I saw Pierre shift in his chair. "Here's the thing: this doctor had HIV himself, and he didn't tell her, even though he insisted they have unprotected sex. She only found out months later, when she discovered antiretroviral drugs in his bathroom. By then, she also had the virus.

"She laid a charge of murder against him. The judge found him guilty, saying that, as there's no cure for HIV, he had effectively handed her a death sentence."

Sensing that I had identified the moral of the story, I piped up, "But that's only because he knew his status, right? So, as long as you don't get tested, you're in the clear. Ignorance is legal bliss. Cheers!" I raised my glass and took a sip.

Daniel swung around. "But don't you see how *wrong* that is?"

I lowered my glass in surprise. "What do you mean? Nobody is *obliged* to get tested. And if someone sleeps with you without inquiring about your status, they've accepted the wager, haven't they? They're probably a risky lay themselves!"

"I agree, but sometimes," he said, glancing at Pierre, "the only reason a girl doesn't inquire about your status is because she trusts you, and if you know this, and that she's innocent herself, you'd be cruel to put her at risk."

"You're speaking a lot of sense there, old boy. I've never been in that situation myself, but I've faced a similar test, which, if I may say so, I passed quite admirably." I shifted forward in my chair and grew a grin. "Early last year, I went home with this little Danish blonde. I kid you not, the moment I closed the bedroom door, she ordered me to take off my pants. 'Take off your pants!' Just like that.

"Anyway, gentleman that I am, I obliged the lady. She—a nurse—then went down on her haunches and started inspecting my goods. After making a few favorable comments, she asked if I had any diseases.

"'No!' I cried, shocked.

"'AIDS?'

"'Highly unlikely.'

"'But you live in South Africa. Everybody has AIDS here.'

"So I countered with a rather nifty non sequitur: 'Are you telling me nobody has AIDS in Denmark?'

"She acknowledged that they do—she looks after some of them. After a triumphant 'well then' from me, she moaned about how badly she wanted to suck my cock. So I told her, 'Suck it, then.' But as I shuffled toward her like a limbo dancer, she jumped back onto the AIDS horse: 'Are you *sure* you don't have AIDS?'

"And then I told what I think was close to the perfect white lie. 'Yeah, yeah,' I said. 'I got tested last year.'

"'Really?' she said, impressed. 'And how many girls have you been with since?'

"'Not many,' I said. And then, as I filled her mouth, I added, 'But I've been safe. Really. I think it's important. I do.'"

I beamed up at Daniel.

"What the fuck?"

"What?"

"You're sick!"

"What do you mean?"

"You lied to her!"

"Yes, but don't you see how brilliantly? I not only

made a believable statement. I also managed to inform her that, if she were to wrap her lips around my member, she'd still be running a risk."

"But you didn't inform her *properly!* What about all the girls you'd been with before your so-called 'test'? Do you think she still would've taken the risk if she had known about them?"

I made my number-crunching face, then dropped my head in shame.

"I see your point, old boy."

I couldn't see him at present (head being dropped), but I suspect he was eyeing me with a fair bit of frustration when he said, "How the fuck did you become a psychologist?"

"Hey now!" I cried out, looking up. "Don't insult me. I'm only human. It's not easy spotting your own flaws, especially when getting laid depends on not spotting them." I took a shaky sip of whisky. "That said, I *have* bedded a bordello load of questionable pussy, so it really should have been clearer to me that my caveat to the Dane was insufficient."

His face contorted. "And then you sleep with Layla? Do you know how *innocent* she was?"

"Well, after tonight I do, but not before. We met in a club, we hooked up. No questions asked. For all I knew, she was the dirtiest slut in Cape Town."

"But she wasn't!"

"I didn't know that. I had no idea where she had been."

Puffing up like a preacher in the pulpit, he pointed a trembling finger and shouted, "But you knew where *you* had been! You knew!"

Hitherto, the lad hadn't once genuinely gotten on my nerves, but this vulgar hypocrisy, I admit, injected a generous dose of bona fide bite into my response.

Eyeing him sharply, I said, "And you, old boy? Don't you also know where *you* have been?"

It took a heartbeat for the mirror I'd held up to do its work. I watched the color drain from his face as he realized his moral high ground had vaporized and he was standing at eye level with me. He collapsed onto an ottoman.

No sooner had he hit the velvet than I heard hurried footsteps. Layla came rushing through the door like a flustered ostrich, crying out, "I didn't sleep with him, Daniel! I promise! He's lying!"

"What the fuck?" I blurted out, eyeing the ceiling. How did she overhear us?

"It doesn't matter," said Daniel. He stared blankly ahead, his preacher's fire extinguished.

"But really, I didn't!"

"I believe you." He transferred his hollow gaze to her.

He eyed her for a second, then stood up and moved toward the door. "Come with me."

She scuttled after him.

I watched them exit, then followed at a discreet distance, pausing only to pat Pierre on the back. The man looked as though he'd been struck by lightning. I trailed them to the kitchen, where I loitered by the door and peeked in.

"No, why? Why do you say that?" Layla cried out. "I promise, we didn't do anything!"

"It's not about that," said Daniel. "I've told you already, I believe you. I just can't be with you right now. I'm a mess. I'm no good for you. No good for anybody."

"That's not true!"

"It is! Trust me. There are things about me that you don't know, things that would change your mind."

"Like what? Tell me."

"No."

"Tell me!"

"Please, Layla. Just let it go."

"Tell me!"

"No! Just go!"

Sensing that negotiations had broken down and that a departure was imminent, I withdrew. The last thing I heard was Daniel saying, "I'll get you a cab."

Evidently not taking him up on his offer, Layla burst

into the hallway just as I slid back into the drawing room. And scarcely had I set foot in the room, dear reader, when I screeched to a halt, and my eyeballs lunged out of their sockets like cuckoo clocks. For, believe it or not, Pierre had left his chair and was now on the floor, butt pointing east-north-east and nose nuzzling the carpet. I quickly gathered that he was in conversation with The Big Man—pleading with him, to be more precise.

"I'm so sorry, God, I'm so sorry," he whimpered. "Please forgive me, please. I love her so much, God. I love her so much. Please, please, I can't." By the time he had said "I can't", his voice had been reduced to a squeak. A remarkable thing, considering his size. And deprived of his ability to form vowels, he stooped to wailing: loud, slobbering, cheek-wobbling wailing. Picture, if you will, a firetruck in mourning.

Thankfully, this racket lasted only a few seconds. Quite unexpectedly, he checked it. He stopped swaying to and fro, and after a pause, addressed the Lord with a vigor and a Sean Connery quality of voice I wouldn't have thought possible moments earlier.

"My help comes from the Lord," he started in a rich baritone, "the maker of heaven and earth. He will not let your foot slip. He who keeps you will not slumber. Indeed, He who watches over Israel will neither slumber nor sleep. The Lord watches over you. The Lord is your shade at your right hand. The sun will not harm you by day, nor the moon by night. The Lord will keep you from all harm; He will watch your life …"

Daniel suddenly swooped past me and, squatting down in front of Pierre like a strongman, first toppled him onto his side, causing an earthquake, before rolling him onto his back. Then he straddled him and, grabbing him by the chest, shouted, "Pierre! Pierre! Look at me! This won't help! Do you hear me? This won't help! You have to get tested. If you want to be with my sister, you have to get tested!"

Daniel shook Pierre like a backpack he was trying to rid of sand. After one particularly violent shake, the divine fire seemed to desert the believer. His eyes grew moist and fearful.

"I am scared, Daniel."

Daniel's grip slackened.

"So am I. But we have to do it."

He collapsed onto the floor.

I stepped forward.

"Yes," I said, looking all sorry and shaking my head, "we have to. This has gone on for too long—way too long. It's time to do the right thing." I picked up my keys. "I'm going now. Daniel, Pierre—it's been a pleasure. Stay strong." I thumped my chest two times and withdrew.

When I stepped onto the porch and took a big lungful of night air, I felt like a newborn—fresh from the womb, with the whole world and all its fabulous possibilities splayed out before me. I was buzzing. What a night! What a story! I broke into a waltz, prancing like Count Vronsky before toddling down the steps toward the gate.

Once out, I launched into yet another rotation, but aborted the maneuver halfway when the sound of a piano reached my ears. Daniel was playing something quite beautiful, I must admit. *Pavane pour une infante défunte*, I later learned.

I noticed something else: the balcony door above the drawing room stood open. Layla must've eavesdropped from there.

Speaking of the lass, when I reached my car, I spotted her forlorn figure some way down the road. Thinking that I might just as well have a crack at her—I mean, she was on the way—I swung the carriage around and chased her down.

Leaning over to the passenger window, I said, "Layla, old girl, let me give you a lift home. You don't know how dangerous this area has become. Just the other day, an old lady and her dog got hacked to death.* Come, get in."

"Leave me alone," she muttered.

"Layla …"

* Not true.

"Just leave me alone!"

"Okay, but just listen to me quickly! Please, just stop for a moment. Layla!"

The verbal rap of the hammer did the trick. She braked, albeit more in the manner of a hostile prisoner of war than a bright-eyed recruit, and turned to me with hard, wet eyes.

"Look," I said, "everything I said back there was a lie—a *lie!* I don't really treat women like that. I only said it to force a breakthrough in Daniel. There was no other way. I'm sorry I involved you, but he simply had to be stopped. He was a danger to society."

The last line hooked her. She rushed to the window and said, "Why do you say that?"

I averted my eyes.

"You know I can't tell you that. Daniel's a client."

She clasped the windowsill.

"Laurence, *please!* You have to tell me! You don't know what this is doing to me."

I fidgeted with the gear lever.

"Okay," I said at last. "But not here. Let me get you home safely, and then we can talk."

She nodded and said, "Do you mind if we pick up my housemate in Long Street? I'm supposed to meet her there."

"Of course not," I said without hesitation.

After all, if things didn't work out with Layla, I could always try my luck with the housemate. She was presumably the one Daniel and Layla had overheard having sex, so she might not be altogether against the idea of a late-night romp with her friend's trusted advisor.

As I pulled away, Layla phoned her to coordinate. The girl agreed to meet us outside Solstice. When we arrived, Layla spotted her at once.

"There she is."

"Where?" I asked, craning to see past her.

"By the lamppost." She pointed out a girl in white. "I'll go get her."

Once she was out and the door had clicked shut, I hastily wound down her window and shouted, "Layla! Got to go! Just got a text—one of my patients. Suicide!"

I sped off. The girl in white was Heidi.

## A Scary Morning ... Some Damn Fine PR

I was still stepping on it like a gangster whose pompadour had been grazed by a bullet when my mind began to connect the tantalizing dots.

The first connection: Heidi had informed Layla of Daniel's whereabouts that evening. After all, Daniel had mentioned to Pierre he'd seen Layla's housemate in the piano lounge. And Heidi had gone up there right after her chant. It stands to reason that she then tipped off Layla.

The second connection—and this one made me positively giddy—involved the night Daniel and Layla overheard her housemate's bedroom gymnastics. If the housemate was Heidi, then it was probably *this author* who ravished the little maniac! Think about it: Heidi stormed into Layla's room and kicked up a fuss about some perceived wrong on the part of her lover. And you remember what happened between us, right?

Now, granted, Heidi probably runs into trouble with just about every lad who makes the potentially life-wrecking decision of sleeping with her. And yet, by comparing Daniel's timeline with my own, I determined the events almost certainly overlapped. But even if it hadn't been me, I thought with a thrill, I'd make it appear so. Yes, the people would like that.

Back in my apartment, I stretched out on my bed and smiled up at the whirring ceiling fan.

What a night, I thought. What a glorious, beautiful night. What I could do with it all. What a story I could write. A play. Yes. Women would love that.

"So, what do you do for a living, Dixon?"

"I'm a playwright."

"A playwright! Wow, how fascinating. What do you write about?"

"Ah, you know, HIV and …"

I bolted upright.

"Fuck!"

A terrible realization had struck me: if I wanted to write a play about this pestilence, I would have to get tested for it myself. There were no two ways about it.

People, especially women, would naturally ask if I'd been tested. And what a silly ass I'd look if I said no. And if I lied, the truth would surely be uncovered. It would be the very first thing a journalist worth their cynical salt would look into. And once the fact had been uncovered, I'd be fucked, well and truly—denounced and ostracized as a hypocrite.

There was no way around it, then. I had to go through with it. Or drop the project. But that was never truly an option. The upside was too dazzling. Just imagine I got tested at the crack of dawn and wrote that up. Imagine how that would make me seem. Like a goddamn hero, I tell you! A beacon of principle and courage! A man among wimps! It would be beautiful. Too beautiful to keep to myself. Unless, of course, I'd thought it likely I would test positive.

Fortunately, I didn't. I had generally been good about wrapping up my boy, no matter how ardently women begged for the full Dixon. In fact, the more they begged, the quicker I reached for the wrapper. With nutjobs like Heidi in particular, I didn't chance it. So I wasn't too concerned.

The next morning, after only about two hours of sleep, I stumbled down to the pharmacy. It wasn't even open yet when I arrived, so I loitered outside until a Larry-David-looking Jew came around the corner and let me in.

He led me to a wooden chair at the back of the shop, hidden behind an upright to spare the occupant embarrassment, and told me to wait while he fetched the kit.

When he returned, he asked if I'd been through the ordeal before. I stammered a "no" and watched as he swabbed my index finger and pricked it. Having sucked up a few incriminating drops of blood, he pressed them into the tester on the table. He explained the geometry of my future: one red line meant I was fine; two meant I was fucked. He draped a tissue over the device with a funereal seriousness I could have done without and suggested I get some air.

I wandered up a nearby sunny street, sat on the curb, and endured fifteen minutes of paranoia and the barks of a vindictive dog. Finally, my foundations wobbling dangerously, I got up and took the plunge.

I stumbled back into the shop with a let's-just-get-it-over-with urgency. Without waiting for the man, I stormed the table and lifted the tissue with a trembling hand. I reeled. The pharmacist arrived a moment later.

"You're fine," he said. "You can settle up front."

Thank fuck, I thought.

When I got home, I went straight to work. I guzzled a pot of coffee and began transcribing my recordings. I documented it all—the City Hall circus, the tryst with Heidi, the squabble with Yvonne—before shifting into PR mode. I began shaping the narrative to make me look like a flawed but ultimately well-intentioned hero.

For example, my alterations to the scene where I

convince Layla to let me drive her home. In reality, I had told her that my utterances in Daniel's drawing room were mere lies designed to help him see the error of his ways, thus denying both my story about the Danish nurse and my own supposed ethical breakthrough.

In the play, I'd simply offer to make a clean breast of it, to tell her everything she wanted to know about Daniel and myself. On the condition, of course, that she'd let me take her home, because I wouldn't be able to live with myself if, god forbid, something were to happen to her on those dangerous, dangerous streets.

I made a few other tweaks, but on the whole, I let things be. People will swallow a mountain of bullshit if it contains a pebble of truth.

I spent a week cleaning the thing up, and then it was off to the market. Pitched it, sold it, and landed the role of—you guessed it—myself. Or rather, Richard: the heroic sexual dynamo based on me. Three months later, it was opening night.

Proceed!

## Specters of the Past ... A Glorious Disaster

In the weeks leading up to this momentous evening, I spent a fair bit of time trying to envisage how it might go wrong. I did so to prevent the trouble I could and, at the bare butt minimum, brace for the trouble I couldn't. *Premeditatio malorum*, the Stoics called it—the premeditation of evils.

Despite these altogether fruitful efforts, I'm not embarrassed to admit that I failed spectacularly in anticipating the outcome. For one, I did not foresee that, merely minutes before stepping onstage, I'd be kibitzing with Heidi. Yes, Heidi. Looney-Tunes Heidi.

This unfortunate encounter came about because I had to run down to the lobby to hand over tickets to Yvonne, who had been unable to pick them up from me that afternoon. We were an item now, by the way.

After that night at Crazy Joe's, we didn't speak for a week. I was too busy working on the play. Experience had also taught me that, in defeat, the best way forward is often to retreat. And so it proved to be. She texted me the following weekend, saying she wanted to meet. Needless to say, I displayed none of the defensive lunacy of the previous weekend. I was back to my cool, effortless self and casually told her about my play. Boy, was she impressed. Went home with me that same night.

Now I found her waiting for me at the foot of the staircase in the theater's lobby, looking sultry as hell. Annette lurked nearby. I had given up on the idea of separating them.

Handing her the tickets, I said, "Am I seeing you afterward?"

She grinned cheekily and said, "Depends on how good it is."

"It's going to be good alright!" I said, pulling her in for a kiss. And just as our lips were about to meet, a large shape entered my peripheral vision. It was Heidi, emerging from the throng of wine-sipping patrons with a look of delighted wonder on her face. I let go of Yvonne.

"Vicar of Christ."

She turned to see what had spooked me and said, "Who is that?"

"Heidi."

"*The* Heidi?"

"Yes."

"Oooh." She turned back to me. "She's not going to be happy with this." She squeezed my hand. "Annette and I are getting drinks. Good luck!" She pecked me on the cheek and left, chuckling merrily when Heidi glared at her in passing.

Heidi swiftly reassumed her goofy expression and, to my grand astonishment, opened her arms as though she thought we were going to hug.

"Dixon!" she started. "So good to—"

I halted her progress with a stiff right arm and said, "What the hell are you doing here?"

"I came to see your play, of course."

"And that's all? Just came to see my play? Not to make a scene? How did you even find out about it?"

"My housemate mentioned it."

I froze.

"Your housemate?"

"She wanted to see it, and when I saw your name on the poster, I thought—"

"Where is she?"

"My housemate? In the restroom. Why?"

"I have to go."

I wheeled around and started up the stairs.

"Good luck! Let's meet afterward?"

"I have plans."

"With that girl?"

"Yes."

"Another time, then. She doesn't have to know."

"No, but I'll have to."

In hindsight, I can't say I was surprised our marketing material had hooked Layla. We had infused the copy with just enough ambiguity for her to imagine the play was a godsend—something she could relate to, something written specifically for her. What concerned me was how she'd react when she realized it was written *about* her.

This was for two reasons. First—and this may come as somewhat of a surprise—I felt a twinge of guilt about embroiling her in my schemes. She was a nice girl, after all, and I didn't wish her any further suffering, which was the inevitable outcome of her watching the play. I mean, how would *you* feel about paying good money to watch a public re-enactment of your love life, only to learn that you've also been played for a fool? A lot of things, I imagine, and none of them pleasant.

One thing you might feel, and this brings me to my second point, is a desire for revenge. I was worried she might want to get back at me.

Now, I know what you're thinking: what about Heidi? Wasn't she more likely to seek vengeance, given her monstrous personality? To which I'd say, yes, of course.

The thing is, she no longer had any sway over me. Our interactions were in the public domain now, included word-for-word in the play. They were, therefore, useless as kompromat. Yvonne, for one, didn't mind them; she considered them the height of hilarity.

The same could not be said of the dirt that Layla had on me—or, rather, the dirt that she was about to have on me. See, by watching the play, she would discover how I'd reimagined our final interactions to suit my image. She alone would know where the truth ended and my fabrications began, and she alone could call me out on it … if she were so inclined.

Ultimately, I deemed it unlikely. Her personality didn't allow for it. She was too soft, too self-effacing, far more likely to be consumed by her own pain than the pain she could exact on me.

By the time I reached the wings, I had successfully filed her away as a non-threat. I stepped onto the stage with a sense of ease and lost myself in the work. I was magnificent. For nearly ninety minutes, I delivered a blemish-free performance to an audience that seemed to be breathing in unison with me.

Then we reached the second-to-last scene—the cre-scendo of my reimagined heroism. It's the scene where I try to convince Layla (played by Cecille Schoeman, whom I was fornicating with on the side) to let me give her a lift home. I was just leaning into a particularly poignant line, savoring the hushed, reverent silence of the house, when our peace was shattered.

A door at the back of the house was violently kicked open, the crash echoing through the auditorium like a gunshot.

Jesus Christ, I thought, she's gone off her rocker!

I kept my wits about me, stayed in character. If it really had been Layla, I reasoned, she was gone now. She wouldn't be heard from again, at least not tonight.

The cast followed my lead. Cecille, after the briefest of halts, finished her line; Tommaso continued his rendition of *Pavane pour une infante défunte*; and Simon remained on the floor near the piano, his face fixed in an expression of grave, thoughtful sorrow. Only the patrons broke rank, their heads swinging around in unison to investigate.

A moment later, a voice thundered from the shadows beneath the balcony: "You fucker!"

I knew at once I had misread the situation. It wasn't Layla who had disrupted our peace; it was this man. And in the wake of his opening broadside, our professional poise evaporated.

Tommaso flubbed a note—though, to his credit, he soldiered on—while the rest of us turned to face the intruder. At first, he was little more than a distant silhouette framed by the blood-red glow of an EXIT sign. But he was closing in, stomping down the aisle, his voice booming: "I trusted you! I confided in you! And you do *this?*"

As he spat the last word, he stepped out from the darkness of the balcony and into the ghostly blue light of the stage-front.

It was Daniel.

To this day, I don't know how he found out about the play, or why he chose this most extraordinary time and place to air his grievances about it. My best guess is that an acquaintance in the audience had slipped him a text. He then dropped whatever he was busy with and, while evidently growing into the sort of rage that ought to have caused local policemen to sit up and take notice, raced down to the theater.

Whatever the case may be, I was stunned. I had, as I explained earlier, done my utmost to imagine every way this evening could go south, but not even in my most creative of moods had I conjectured something so preposterous. My worst fear was that the man might accost me late at night, outside my home—not in a fucking theater.

Yet there he was, coming down the aisle like a blood-thirsty gladiator. He was clearly in a blinding rage, which explained why he pitched up to begin with; he was blind to all social and professional considerations. But this is neither here nor there. What mattered was that he was there, he was incensed, and he was closing in on me. To a sensible mind like my own, it suggested I had to act—and act quickly.

I didn't feel the urge immediately, though. I was kind of paralyzed, muttering something like "What the..." while Cecille hissed, "Who is that?" But as he advanced and the sheer scale of his rage became more apparent, I sensed he wouldn't conclude his trip until he was close enough to count my eyelashes—a scenario I preferred to avoid.

So, without further delay, I stepped forward and opened my arms in a grand, conciliatory gesture. "Daniel, old boy," I said warmly.

In retrospect, "old boy" was perhaps not the mot juste, because he responded by yelling "Fuck your old boy!" and charging the stage.

"Sorry, old boy!" I yelled. "But you need to calm down!"

"Fuck you!"

"The story had to get out! It's for the greater good! It might *save* people!"

By now, he was clambering onto the stage. I considered scramming, but a quick cost-benefit analysis suggested it would be a strategic error. I'd lose too much face. Had the auditorium been empty, I'd have been half-way up Table Mountain by now, but with Yvonne and the who's who of Cape Town in the crowd, I'd have to stand my ground. At the very least, I could crab-walk a few meters to the left to put the piano between us, in the hope that either Tommaso or Simon would intervene before he reached me.

A naive hope. These two cowards did absolutely nothing. As Daniel crested the stage, Simon scrambled up from the floor and retreated to protect his own skin—as though he were important enough to be a target—while Tommaso, who for some perverse artistic reason had continued playing Ravel up to that point, simply turned his head to watch the carnage.

I, meanwhile, kept trying to subdue the flames: "Calm down, old boy! Calm down!"

It was to no avail. If anything, it spurred him on. As he cleared the piano, a hellish glint entered his eyes, and I began to brace for impact. I shifted my right foot back and dropped into a slight squat to establish a stronger base, raising my hands to chest height.

After discharging one final, uninspired jibe ("You fucking cunt!"), we clashed. He likely wanted to take a whack at me from the start, but I suspect he noticed the easy athleticism of my stance—I was a pro cricketer once, after all—and realized that such a bold opening statement would get him nowhere. Instead, he lunged at me like an amateur wrestler, attempting to seize my torso and topple me. I responded in kind. And as we grappled, he resumed his verbal assault, promising to kill me among other bizarre threats, to which I could only repeat my refrain: "Calm down, old boy! Calm down! Calm down!" That is, until I thought of something a little more eloquent: a quote from *Hamlet*.

I had discovered it a few days earlier and earmarked it for future interviews. Now seemed as good a time as ever to debut it. "Remember what Hamlet said, old boy! 'The play's the thing wherein I'll—aaargh!'"

The bugger had gotten in underneath me. He ducked, hooked his arms around my legs, and hoisted me into the air before bringing me down onto my back. And when I say he "brought me down onto my back", don't go running off with the idea that he lowered me to the floor like a family heirloom. No, he drove me into the boards with everything he had, knocking the wind out of me. As I lay there groaning, and Cecille screamed "Stop it! Stop it!", he mounted me like a broncobuster and clocked me a big one on the jaw. Then he hit me again—this time on the nose—shattering it.

I don't remember much of what followed—life had become rather fuzzy, as you might imagine—but witnesses who hadn't been punched in the face informed me that just as he was about to strike a third time, Cecille grabbed his arm and held him back heroically.

Her cowardly co-stars at last came to her aid and, between them, removed the maniac from my vitals. While Cecille tended to my remains, Simon and Tommaso restrained him a while longer. When they eventually released him, Tommaso—ever the artist—asked, "You're Daniel, right?"

Daniel nodded, still fixing me with a homicidal eye.

"How did it go with the test?"

I mean, what a ridiculous thing to ask! Then again, on the day I met him, this Italian émigré asked me for Daniel's home address. Why? So he could go interview the man to "get to the root of his being". I nearly puked!

Daniel savored the sight of my bloody face a moment longer, then turned on his heel. As he walked offstage, he grunted, "It doesn't matter. It shouldn't matter."

The O-mouthed stage manager watched him pass, then finally mastered her sweaty self and ordered the curtain down. And as that wall of black dropped into place, dear reader, something truly astonishing happened—something that, if you're unfamiliar with this story, will likely surprise you as much as it did me. A man in the front row burst into applause. Loud, raucous, solitary applause. Can you conceive of such a thing?

There was evidently not a doubt in his mind that

what he had just witnessed was—to quote Jacques Stevens of the *Table Bay Herald*—a "meta-masterpiece". It didn't end there. Soon the rest of the mob joined in and, once the outline of a consensus had formed, the shouting began: "Whooooooooooo!" "Bravo!" "Brilliant!"

This had a most vitalizing effect on me. I shot up like a jack-in-the-box and hurried the cast into position for a curtain call. When the veil lifted, I—bloody-faced, crooked-nosed, but beaming—led the procession back out into the bright, wondrous lights.

The crowd roared at the sight of me. I lifted my left arm triumphantly and, after letting it tower there for a glorious moment, collapsed into a dramatic bow. I snapped back to the vertical only to fall into yet another. Then I thanked the rest of the cast with a sidelong flourish, after which we joined hands and bowed in unison.

As we rose and stood there, gazing out over that fluttering sea of beaming faces, I spotted a slender, dark-haired woman hurrying up the aisle toward the same door Daniel had breached minutes earlier. Layla.

We bowed again.

## A Sad Farewell

"Daring, devastating, sensational!" "A smart, serious drama for our times." "Thompson speaks the truth." "Thompson bares his soul." *Thompson bares his soul?* That last one just about killed me.

The reviews, barring one piece of excrement I'll get to shortly, were tremendous. They also revealed that hardly anyone realized it was the real Daniel who had punched me. They mistook the fracas for part of the act: a kind of meta-theatrical commentary. Rolling with the punches, as it were, the director and I incorporated the scene into future performances. Not until recently did the truth become more widely known, and far from hurting us, it has made a beautiful splash.

The opening night after-party was held in the garden terrace of Upper Kloof. String lights, champagne, the usual. Yvonne was by my side, her hand discreetly on my ass as I accepted congratulations from a parade of well-wishers. My nose was crooked and bruised, but my spirits were soaring.

At one point, a French critic approached me—thick glasses, pretentious scarf, the works.

"I loved it," he declared. "Spectacular."

He kissed me on both cheeks. I thanked him in his native tongue.

Then he asked: "Le point culminant—the climax—was it planned?" He gestured at his own nose. "It looks broken."

"Monsieur," I said, "an artist must suffer for his craft. Even if only for one night."

His eyes widened. "Merveilleux!" Another round of kisses, and he was off.

The following morning, I sat shirtless at my kitchen table, hands clasped behind my head, basking in the glow of victory. Yvonne sat across from me, reading from the newspaper.

"This is a smart, serious drama for our times," she read, "one that fearlessly explores how men navigate desire and responsibility. Not just another merchant of escapism, Thompson delivers a Kafkaesque blow to the frozen male conscience, putting himself on the line in the process."

Kafkaesque. I liked that.

But not everyone was so perceptive. That bald prick

Levi Stavropoulos saw fit to play the contrarian. I shared a few choice snippets earlier: "comically ignorant" and a "kind of accidental Moses", he called me. Then there was this gem: "Thompson's depiction of HIV as a death sentence requiring either celibacy or suicide is not merely outdated but irresponsible. One wonders if he has consulted a medical professional this decade."

*Consulted a medical professional?* What would Levi Stavropoulos know about the terror of HIV? The man is almost certainly still a virgin.

As for Daniel and Layla, I haven't seen either of them since that magnificent evening. Did Layla rush out of the theater to make up with him? Or just to perforate his back with a nail file? I could see either happening. Perhaps she just wanted to get away from it all. The more compassionate side of me would like to believe that the truth set her free. It has that effect, they say … among other, less pleasant ones.

And now, sadly, dear readers, I need to bid you adieu. It's strange to think of it, but this will likely be the last you hear from me. I can picture your face: the distraught expression, the tears welling in your eyes, the trembling lower lip. It pains me, but I can offer you no consolation. This will hurt—like when Dumbledore died.

Farewell, my friends. Farewell.

## The Real Dixon Thompson

George and Margaret sit across from one another at Dixon's kitchen table. The afternoon light has faded to dusk. Neither has moved to turn on a light.

Margaret's eyes are wide with shock.

George sets down the final page and removes his reading glasses. He rubs the bridge of his nose, exhaling a long, weary breath.

Margaret opens her mouth as if to speak, then closes it again.

Finally, George looks up at his wife.

"I told you he was a plonker."